This ELMER BOOK belongs to:

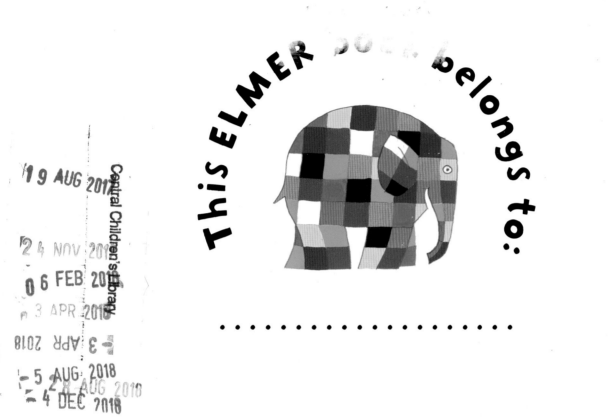

. . . .

For Philippa P.

This paperback first published in 2013 by Andersen Press Ltd.
First published in Great Britain in 2012 by Andersen Press Ltd.,
20 Vauxhall Bridge Road, London SW1V 2SA.
Published in Australia by Random House Australia Pty.,
Level 3, 100 Pacific Highway, North Sydney, NSW 2060.
Text and illustrations copyright © David McKee, 2012
The rights of David McKee to be identified as the author and illustrator
of this work have been asserted by him in accordance with
the Copyright, Designs and Patents Act, 1988.
All rights reserved.
Colour separated in Switzerland by Photolitho AG, Zürich.
Printed and bound in Malaysia by Tien Wah Press.
David McKee has used gouache in this book.

10   9   8   7   6   5   4   3   2   1

British Library Cataloguing in Publication Data available.

ISBN 978 1 84939 688 2

This book has been printed on acid-free paper

ELMER,
ROSE and SUPER EL

David McKee

Andersen Press

Elmer, the patchwork elephant, his cousin, Wilbur, and some other animals were listening to a distant noise. "Sounds like your chaps are having fun, Elmer," said Lion. "What's going on?"

"I have no idea," said Elmer. "That sounds like elephants, but not our herd. Let's find out, Wilbur."

The noise was indeed coming from a herd of elephants, *pink* elephants. They were celebrating the one-hundredth birthday of their oldest elephant, Old. Old himself was leading the herd. Beside him was Rose, a young friend of Elmer's.

Noisily, the elephants made their way to their special clearing near a cliff top. Old went to the highest point close to the edge and faced the herd. Rose gave Old a flower and said, "Happy Birthday!" That was the signal.

"Happy Birthday, ONE," shouted the elephants all together as they stamped their feet. "Happy Birthday, TWO." STAMP! "Happy Birthday, THREE." The elephants intended to shout, stamp and count right up to one hundred. They stamped as one and the ground shook. Poor Rose was so frightened by the noise that she ran off.

But a herd of elephants stamping is like an earthquake. The ground split. The elephants ran back in fear - all except Old, who was left stranded on a pillar of rock. Rose ran into the jungle shouting, "Help! Help!"

Meanwhile Elmer and Wilbur were still on their way to find out what all the noise was about, when suddenly, from opposite directions two smaller elephants appeared.

Elmer knew them both. "Hello, Rose. Hello, Super El,"
he said. "What's the trouble, Rose?"
Rose quickly explained.

"This sounds like a job for me," said Super El.
With that he zoomed off into the air like a rocket.
Rose rushed after him.
"There's nothing we can do," said Elmer. "Let's
go where we can see without being seen."

Super El arrived just as the rock pillar where Old stood started to crumble.

"Please, sir, lift up your trunk," said Super El.

"Hold on, here I come."

Super El caught hold of Old by the trunk and lifted him to safety, just as the rock pillar collapsed.

"Amazing! Fantastic! Wonderful! Extraordinary! Hurrah!" shouted the elephants.

"Thank you," said Old. "Thanks for getting help, Rose. Thank you, Super El. It's been the most exciting and special birthday I've ever had!"
"Please, Super El," said Rose. "When it's my birthday may I have a ride?"

"Why wait until your birthday?" said Super El. "What's wrong with now? Hold my cape tightly. Here we go!" Rose squealed with delight as they took off. After a loop or two to impress the other elephants, they disappeared into the distance.

On the way home Wilbur said, "I hope *our* hundredth birthdays will be special."
"As Super El said, 'What's wrong with now?'" smiled Elmer.
"All days are pretty special really."

Read more ELMER stories

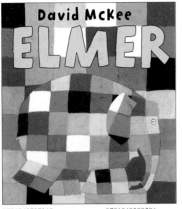

David McKee
ELMER

9781842707319 (paperback)   9781849399296 (eBook)
Also available as a book and CD

David McKee
ELMER AGAIN

9781842707500 (paperback)   9781849399371 (eBook)
Also available as a book and CD

ELMER in the Snow
David McKee

9781842707838 (paperback)   9781849399418 (eBook)
Also available as a book and CD

ELMER and WILBUR
David McKee

9781842709504 (paperback)   9781849399388 (eBook)
Also available as a book and CD

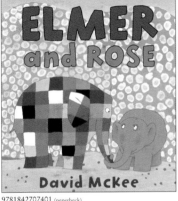

ELMER and ROSE
David McKee

9781842707401 (paperback)

David McKee
ELMER on Stilts

9781842708385 (paperback)   9781849399401 (eBook)

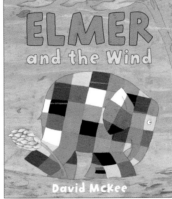

ELMER and the Wind
David McKee

9781842707739 (paperback)   978184939-9432 (eBook)

ELMER and the LOST TEDDY
David McKee

9781842707494 (paperback)

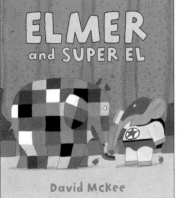

ELMER and SUPER EL
David McKee

9781849394574 (paperback)   9781849399289 (eBook)

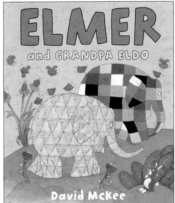

David McKee
ELMER and the HIPPOS

9781842709818 (paperback)   9781849399500 (eBook)

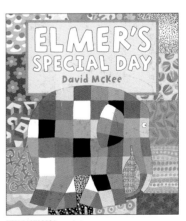

ELMER and GRANDPA ELDO
David McKee

9781842708392 (paperback)   9781849399449 (eBook)

ELMER'S SPECIAL DAY
David McKee

9781842709856 (paperback)

Elmer titles are also available as colour eBooks and Apps.

Find out more about David McKee and Elmer, visit:

www.andersenpress.co.uk